MW01041049

Mr. Cookie Baker

COOKIES

GOOD
MORNING!
Open at 9am

Mr. Cookie Baker

MONICA WELLINGTON

DUTTON CHILDREN'S BOOKS

Baking Supplies

DUTTON CHILDREN'S BOOKS
A division of Penguin Young Readers Group

Published by the Penguin Group
Penguin Group (USA) Inc., 375 Hudson Street, New York, New York 10014, U.S.A.
Penguin Group (Canada), 90 Eglinton Avenue East, Suite 700, Toronto, Ontario, Canada M4P 2Y3
(a division of Pearson Penguin Canada Inc.) • Penguin Books Ltd, 80 Strand, London WC2R 0RL,
England • Penguin Ireland, 25 St Stephen's Green, Dublin 2, Ireland (a division of Penguin Books Ltd)
Penguin Group (Australia), 250 Camberwell Road, Camberwell, Victoria 3124, Australia (a division
of Pearson Australia Group Pty Ltd) • Penguin Books India Pvt Ltd, 11 Community Centre,
Panchsheel Park, New Delhi - 110 017, India • Penguin Group (NZ), Cnr Airborne and
Rosedale Roads, Albany, Auckland 1310, New Zealand (a division of Pearson New Zealand Ltd)
Penguin Books (South Africa) (Pty) Ltd, 24 Sturdee Avenue, Rosebank, Johannesburg 2196,
South Africa • Penguin Books Ltd, Registered Offices: 80 Strand, London WC2R 0RL, England

Copyright © 1992, 2006 by Monica Wellington
All rights reserved.

CIP Data is available.

Published in the United States by Dutton Children's Books,
a division of Penguin Young Readers Group
345 Hudson Street, New York, New York 10014
www.penguin.com/youngreaders
Designed by Abby Kuperstock
Manufactured in China
Revised Edition
ISBN 0-525-47763-2
1 3 5 7 9 10 8 6 4 2

The artwork was done in gouache on paper, with details in colored pencil.

For
Joanne Miller,
top-notch
cookie baker,

and for Lydia,
my little
cookie eater.

The author gratefully thanks
Seth Greenberg of William Greenberg
Jr. Desserts, Inc., of New York City,
and Beth Greenspan.

SUGAR

Early in the morning, Mr. Baker gets ready to make cookies.

ONE DOZEN EGGS

Butter

1 Stick
½ CUP

He counts and
measures the
ingredients for
his recipe.

MY RECIPE
Ingredients:
Directions:
1.
2.
3.

SUGAR

½ cup + ½ cup = 1 CUP

He mixes his
cookie dough.

Then he rolls out the dough and cuts out shapes with cookie cutters.

The cookies bake
in the oven.

Out they come,
nicely browned.
What a delicious
smell!

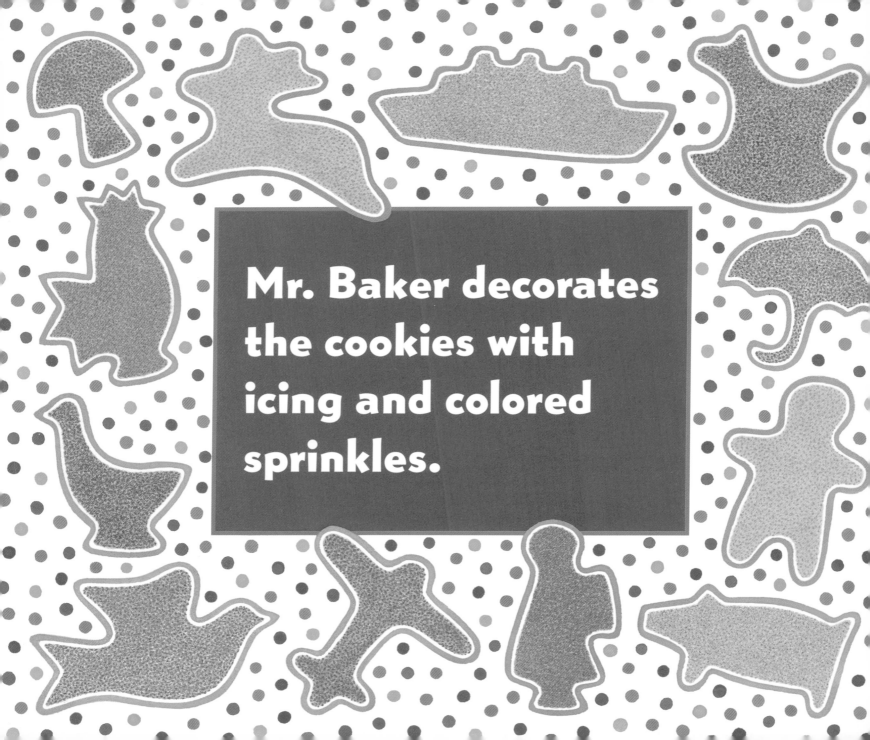

Mr. Baker decorates the cookies with icing and colored sprinkles.

Now he is ready
for customers.
Here come the
hungry children.

Mr. Baker shows
off his cookies.
He is proud.

Mrs. Baker sells the cookies. The shop is crowded.

The cookies are sold. It is time to close.

At last a cookie
for Mr. Baker.
GOOD NIGHT!

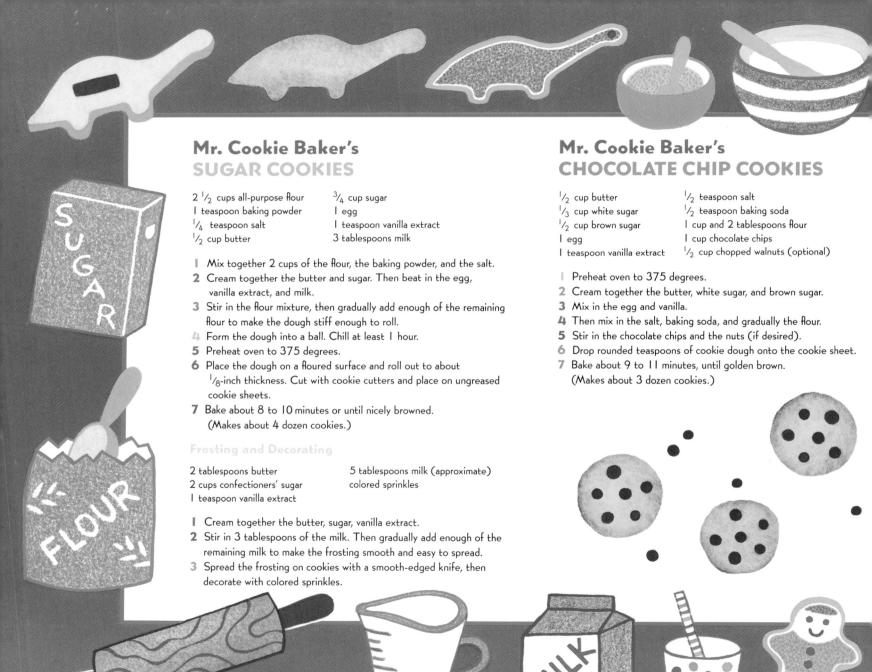

Mr. Cookie Baker's
SUGAR COOKIES

2 ¹/₂ cups all-purpose flour
1 teaspoon baking powder
¹/₄ teaspoon salt
¹/₂ cup butter

³/₄ cup sugar
1 egg
1 teaspoon vanilla extract
3 tablespoons milk

1 Mix together 2 cups of the flour, the baking powder, and the salt.
2 Cream together the butter and sugar. Then beat in the egg, vanilla extract, and milk.
3 Stir in the flour mixture, then gradually add enough of the remaining flour to make the dough stiff enough to roll.
4 Form the dough into a ball. Chill at least 1 hour.
5 Preheat oven to 375 degrees.
6 Place the dough on a floured surface and roll out to about ¹/₈-inch thickness. Cut with cookie cutters and place on ungreased cookie sheets.
7 Bake about 8 to 10 minutes or until nicely browned.
   (Makes about 4 dozen cookies.)

Frosting and Decorating

2 tablespoons butter
2 cups confectioners' sugar
1 teaspoon vanilla extract

5 tablespoons milk (approximate)
colored sprinkles

1 Cream together the butter, sugar, vanilla extract.
2 Stir in 3 tablespoons of the milk. Then gradually add enough of the remaining milk to make the frosting smooth and easy to spread.
3 Spread the frosting on cookies with a smooth-edged knife, then decorate with colored sprinkles.

Mr. Cookie Baker's
CHOCOLATE CHIP COOKIES

¹/₂ cup butter
¹/₃ cup white sugar
¹/₂ cup brown sugar
1 egg
1 teaspoon vanilla extract

¹/₂ teaspoon salt
¹/₂ teaspoon baking soda
1 cup and 2 tablespoons flour
1 cup chocolate chips
¹/₂ cup chopped walnuts (optional)

1 Preheat oven to 375 degrees.
2 Cream together the butter, white sugar, and brown sugar.
3 Mix in the egg and vanilla.
4 Then mix in the salt, baking soda, and gradually the flour.
5 Stir in the chocolate chips and the nuts (if desired).
6 Drop rounded teaspoons of cookie dough onto the cookie sheet.
7 Bake about 9 to 11 minutes, until golden brown.
   (Makes about 3 dozen cookies.)

Mr. Cookie Baker's
PEANUT BUTTER COOKIES

½ cup butter
½ cup white sugar
½ cup brown sugar
½ cup peanut butter
   (creamy or chunky)
1 egg

½ teaspoon vanilla extract
1 tablespoon orange juice
½ teaspoon salt
1 teaspoon baking powder
1 ½ cup flour

1 Preheat oven to 375 degrees.
2 Cream together the butter, white sugar, brown sugar, and peanut butter.
3 Mix in the egg, vanilla, and orange juice.
4 Then mix in the salt, baking powder, and flour.
5 Form the dough into 1-inch balls, place them on the cookie sheet, and
   press them down lightly, marking them with a fork in a crisscross pattern.
   (If the dough is a little sticky, dip the fork in flour.)
6 Bake about 10 to 12 minutes, until lightly browned.
   (Makes about 4 dozen cookies.)

Variation: If you like your cookies even more peanut buttery, keeping
everything else the same, you can add up to a ½ cup more peanut butter.

Mr. Cookie Baker's
OATMEAL COOKIES

½ cup butter
1 cup brown sugar
1 egg
1 tablespoon milk
2 teaspoons cinnamon
½ teaspoon nutmeg

½ teaspoon salt
½ teaspoon baking soda
1 cup flour
1 cup quick-cooking rolled oats
½ cup raisins

1 Preheat oven to 350 degrees.
2 Cream together the butter and brown sugar.
3 Mix in the egg and milk.
4 Then mix in the spices, salt, baking soda, and flour.
5 Stir in the oats, and then the raisins.
6 Drop rounded teaspoons of cookie dough onto greased
   cookie sheet.
7 Bake 8 to 10 minutes, until golden brown.
   (Makes about 3 dozen cookies.)

COOKIES

CLOSED
Good Night